KNOWHERE TO RUN

This edition published 2016 by Paper Rocket
an imprint of Parragon Books Ltd.
Paper Rocket logo and name ™ Parragon Books Ltd

Parragon Books Ltd
Chartist House
15–17 Trim Street
Bath BA1 1HA, UK
www.parragon.com

ISBN 978-1-4748-4510-6

Printed in China

STARRING

STAR-LORD

BY CHRIS "DOC" WYATT

ILLUSTRATED BY

RON LIM AND ANDY TROY

PAPER ROCKET

Stories that take you to another world

FEATURING YOUR FAVOURITES!

STAR-LORD

CAPTAIN MARVEL

COSMO

GAMORA

ROCKET

GROOT

DRAX

ORLANI

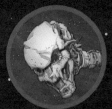

KNOWHERE

THE SKRULL

STAR-LORD'S SHIP

SHI'AR

YON-ROGG

ROBOTIC LIONS

ULTIMATE NULLIFIER

THE STORY OF STAR-LORD

*E*ven when **PETER QUILL** was a little boy on Earth, he always defended people in need. If someone was being picked on at school, Peter stood up for them, even if it meant getting into fights with bullies who were bigger than him. Peter just seemed to have been born with a strong sense of justice.

When he was a little older, Peter finally learned from his mother the truth about his father. Peter's dad was from another planet, called Spartax. His father and mother had met and fallen in love when his father's ship had crashed on Earth.

Knowing that he had a father out in the galaxy drove Peter to reach for the stars. He studied hard in school, designed his own spaceship, and eventually took off from Earth to explore the galaxy!

Many things were very different on the alien worlds Peter visited, but one thing remained the same.... Wherever Peter went he found that there was always some bully who wanted to pick on the little guys. Peter wasn't going to let that happen, no matter what planet he happened to be on.

Peter chose to be a hero! He became –

STAR-LORD!

While fighting to protect the innocent, Star-Lord joined with other heroes from other parts of the cosmos, and together this group became known as the

*F*or the earthling known as **Peter Quill**, life was pretty good on board the space station ***Knowhere***. It was an amazing place, after all. Unlike normal space stations, it wasn't made out of metal or a rare space element. It was made out of bone!

How was that possible? The station was built inside the skull of a long-dead giant celestial being. "I live inside a massive floating alien skull," Peter would say. "How cool is THAT?!"

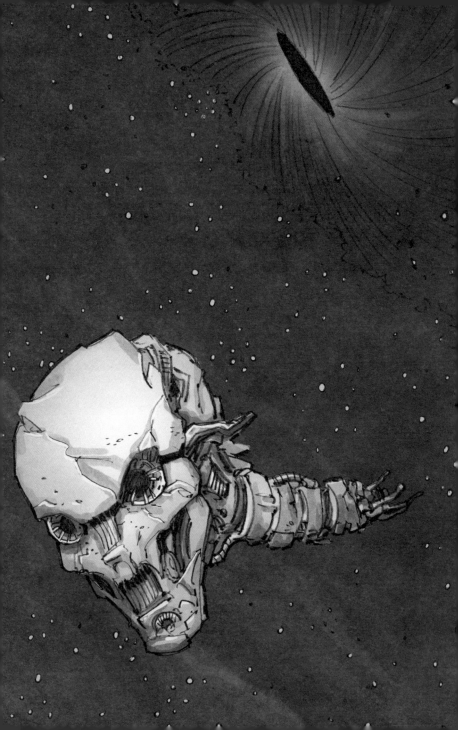

The station was filled with strange and wonderful beings. Peter got to meet people and do things that no other human being ever had, or ever would. It was a pretty special feeling.

But the very best thing about Knowhere was that it served as home base for the

an intergalactic Super Hero team that Peter was proud to be a part of!

There were four other members of the team: **DRAX**, the green-skinned, alien strongman; **GROOT**, a living tree monster from space; *Rocket*, a furry little weapons specialist who looked almost exactly like a large Earth raccoon; and **GAMORA**, an intergalactic warrior trained in several dozen forms of combat. And, of course, there was the leader of the group ...

STAR-LORD.

When he wasn't out in space doing awesome (if sometimes super-dangerous) missions with his team, Peter spent his time doing fun stuff on Knowhere. Take today for example.

This morning Peter went to the Celestial Boot – a restaurant where the Guardians love to hang out – and played space darts with Rocket. "This is going to be a bulls-eye," Rocket shouted as he held up his dart.

"But you're not even aiming at the target," Peter pointed out, holding his dart up as well.

"You'll see," Rocket said. He released his dart, and it zipped around the room, **bouncing** off walls and knocking over people's drinks before landing dead in the target's centre.

> HEY, HOW DID YOU DO THAT?

Rocket showed Peter a tiny device on the tip of his dart. **"Homing beacon,"** Rocket explained. "It will always go where I tell it to, no matter what direction I throw it in – I designed it myself!"

6

WHOOSH!

"Always?" asked Peter. "Let's see about that!" He took the whole box of darts and threw them all at once, scattering them in the air! They WHOOSHED around the restaurant in all directions, causing patrons to duck as the darts pinged and ponged off the plates, the tables, the floor and the ceiling before ...

... they landed, clustered perfectly, in the bullseye of the target!

"AWESOME!"

shouted Peter and Rocket together, high-fiving.

7

Later that day, Peter hung out with all of his other friends.

He did a space race with **Drax,** ran some cool

ZERO-G training exercises with **Gamora,**

and even tried meditating in a garden

with **Groot.**

WOO-HOO!

I'M AS LIGHT AS AIR!

8

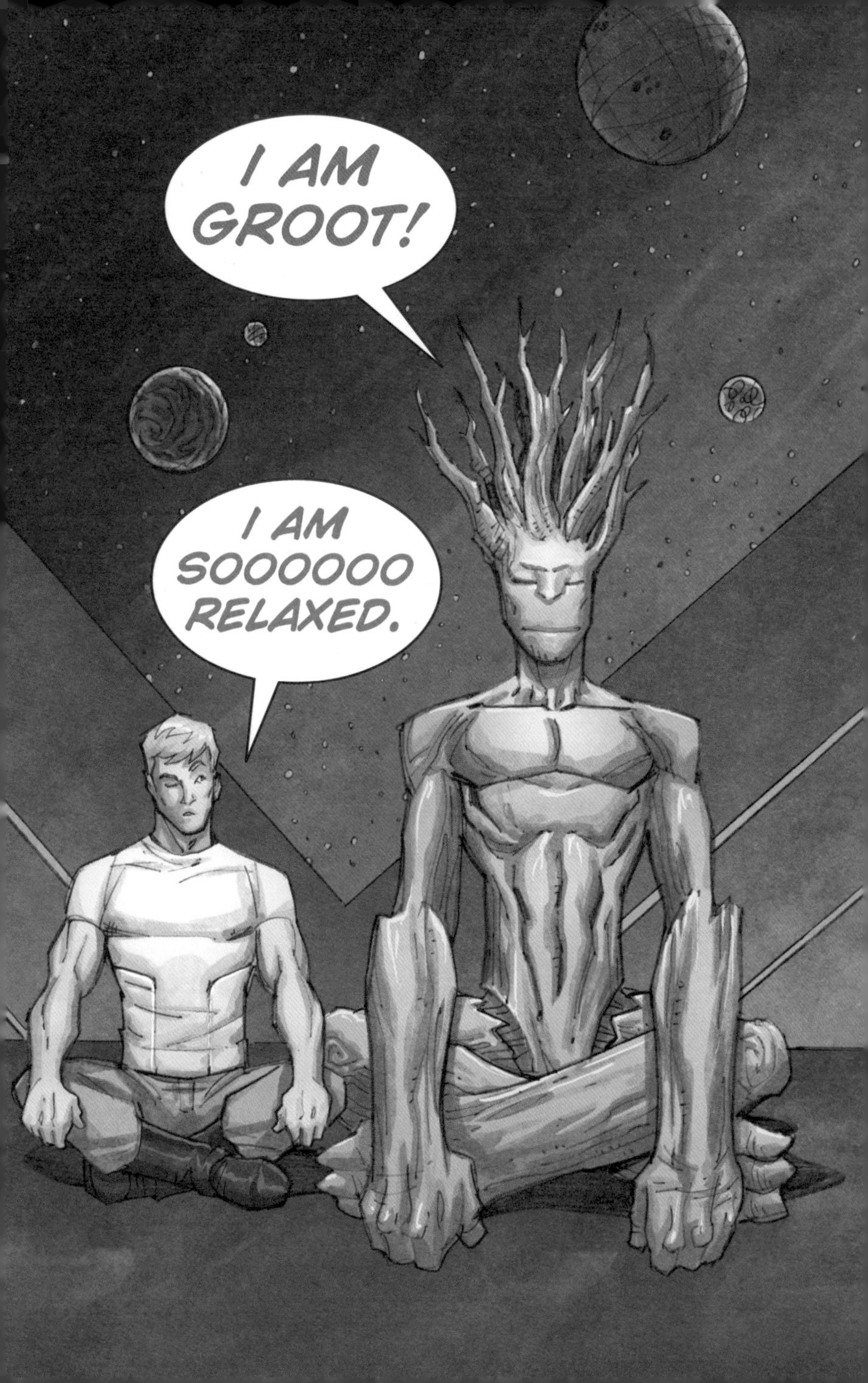
I AM GROOT!
I AM SOOOOOO RELAXED.

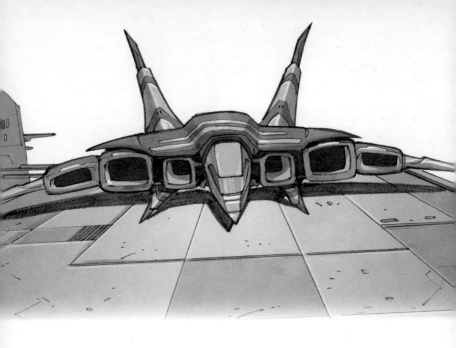

All in all, it was a pretty incredible day. When it was over, Peter headed back home to his bedroom on board his spaceship, which was docked semi-permanently on Knowhere. On his way, he walked past the only other earthling living on Knowhere: Cosmo.

"Good evening, Peter," Cosmo said as he walked past Peter going in the other direction.

"You too, Cosmo," said Peter to the animal. Cosmo was the only other earthling, but Cosmo wasn't a human being. He was a dog! Born in Russia in the 1960s, Cosmo was launched into the galaxy as a cosmonaut, part of the Russian government's experiments in space travel. But Cosmo fell into a wormhole, and he wound up gaining advanced intelligence and mental abilities – including the power to communicate with humans. Now he was head of security on Knowhere.

OH, BY THE WAY ... HAPPY BIRTHDAY, PETER!

That stopped Peter in his tracks. "What?"

"I know that the calendar is different here on Knowhere," said Cosmo. "The days and weeks are different lengths, and there are only eight months in the year and everything.... But I keep an Earth calendar on my desk at work, because it reminds me of home, and I happened to notice that on Earth, right now, it's your birthday."

It was Peter's birthday and he hadn't even realized it!

SAY WHAAAAAT?

*P*eter was bummed out. Back on Earth, he'd loved his birthdays. His mother had always made a lot of fuss for Peter on what she called his "big day". There was a party filled with cake, music and, of course, presents. But more than anything else, there was that warm feeling of being surrounded by friends and family who

clearly loved him and wanted to make things special on his "big day".

And now, so far from home, Peter didn't even notice that his birthday was happening. It had been years since he had gone back to Earth to see his loved ones. Yep, there was no denying it – **Peter was homesick**.

The next day Peter's friends, the Guardians, could tell their leader was down, and they tried to cheer him up. Rocket and Groot took him to the **Orlani Races**.

Orlani

"Nobody can feel bad at the Orlani Races," declared Rocket.

"**I am Groot**," Groot agreed with a slight nod. Groot always said "I am Groot" to everything. Luckily, his best friend Rocket knew just what the tree monster meant.

"**See? He agrees with me**," Rocket confirmed.

Orlani were little creatures – kind of like the alien versions of muskrats or ferrets. For fun, the Orlani were put on a little track and were made to race each other towards the finishing line, as the spectators watched and cheered them on! Everyone picked their favourites and shouted their support.

When the race started, Rocket shouted,

"**Run, Little Brownie!**"

at the Orlani he liked. "**I am Groot,**" Groot added, also trying to encourage Little Brownie.

Despite himself, Peter started to cheer up. But then Little Brownie JUMPED out of the track, and ran straight into the crowd.

"Hey, where's it going?" Peter asked. Suddenly, he felt something weird. Little Brownie was running straight up the leg of Peter's trousers!

"Ahh – ohhh – awww –"

Peter shouted as he jumped around! The Orlani's little claws were scratching and tickling him all at once! "Get this thing off meeeee!" Peter yelled at Rocket and Groot!

It took several minutes to get the Orlani out of his trousers, and the job involved Peter stripping down to his boxers and vest in public. When it was all over, Peter was in a worse mood than ever.

"OKAY, I WAS WRONG," Rocket admitted. **"SOME PEOPLE MIGHT BE ABLE TO FEEL BAD AT THE ORLANI RACES."**

Peter's friends didn't give up trying to cheer him up, though. Gamora took Peter to the space dojo to show him some cool fighting moves. But when Peter tried them, he fell flat on his face!

Later, in an attempt to treat Peter's homesickness, Drax tried cooking an Earth recipe. There was just one problem: having never made or even tasted Earth food before, Drax got the ingredients all mixed up. He ended up making a **chocolate-chicken cake with oyster frosting**. Which, while disgusting to Peter, just so happened to be something Rocket ENJOYED eating!

"Thanks for trying," Peter said to Drax – once he stopped gagging.

VOILA!

Cosmo told Peter that he had just got a shipment of special treats from Earth. He added that he always ate them when he wanted to be reminded of home. The considerate canine wanted to share one with Peter, which got Star-Lord excited – until the special treats turned out to be **DOG TREATS**.

I should have realized, Peter thought as he politely choked down the dry, bone-shaped animal snack.

It was really nice that everyone wanted to help, but Peter put it to them bluntly: "Since none of you are even human, you just can't

understand what I need." Focusing on his own disappointment, he walked back home to his ship, not realizing that he had just hurt his friends' feelings.

But that evening, while on his parked ship, Peter heard a knock on the door. He opened it and saw the last thing he ever expected to see ...

ANOTHER HUMAN!

It was **Captain Marvel**, a Super Hero from Earth!

"Star-Lord, I'm so happy I've found you," she said. "I need your help. In fact, **everyone on Earth needs your help**!"

*P*eter had met Captain Marvel a few times while Iron Man and some of the other Avengers were on a mission against **THANOS**. He knew that Captain Marvel's real name was **Carol Danvers**. She used to be in the United States Air Force, but after receiving an infusion of **ALIEN DNA**, she developed

super powers — including super strength, endurance, stamina, and even the power of flight! She soon joined the AVENGERS and battled alongside Earth's Mightiest Heroes.

Whether she had **part-alien DNA** or not, Peter was so happy to see a fellow human being! He invited her inside immediately.

Once on board his ship, Captain Marvel explained why she was there.

Peter knew the SKRULLS all too well. They were aliens, and many of them were evil and loved war. They had tried to invade Earth on multiple occasions but had always been beaten back by the Avengers and other powerful heroes, such as Spider-Man and Wolverine.

"These SKRULLS were a small team, and they had been searching for something," Captain Marvel went on. "Eventually the Avengers discovered what the alien agents had been after: the pieces needed to rebuild the...

"The Ultimate Nullifier?" Peter asked. "Do you mean the weapon capable of destroying entire solar systems?"

Peter had never seen the Ultimate Nullifier, but he knew that even some of the biggest bad guys in the Universe – like GALACTUS, RONAN and even THANOS himself – were actually afraid of it. To protect the universe, the heroes of Earth had found it and broken the weapon into several pieces, scattering them in secret locations. But if the

SKRULLS were able to put those pieces together again, they'd cause big trouble for sure!

"We captured the whole Skrull team ... except one," said Captain Marvel.

"Let me guess," Peter replied, a chill going down his spine. "The SKRULL who got away is the one who has the pieces to the Ultimate Nullifier."

"Yes," Captain Marvel confirmed. "And I've tracked him – to Knowhere! If that SKRULL agent gets the parts back to his home planet, I'm positive the scientists of his world will be able to put it together again. Once they have a working Ultimate Nullifier, they'll be able to

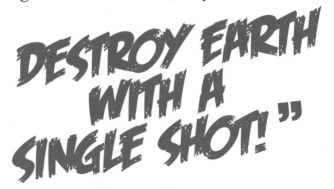 DESTROY EARTH WITH A SINGLE SHOT!"

The words hit Peter like a ton of bricks. His memories of being a child rushed back: playing ball in his yard; battling imaginary monsters from his tree house; reading comic books down by the stream. All of these places would be destroyed. His friends – his family – gone. Peter made a **tight fist**. He wasn't going to let that happen. "We have to stop him before it's too late."

"So, you'll help me, Star-Lord?" Captain Marvel asked.

"You bet I will," Peter responded, grabbing his blaster and helmet. **"Where do we start?"**

"Well, that's where it gets tricky," Captain Marvel responded. "Don't forget – SKRULLS are shape-shifters!"

"Oh ... right," said Peter, remembering. It was true. Every SKRULL alien had the natural ability to change their bodies and make them look like anyone or anything they wanted. It was a form of camouflage that made them great spies and secret agents.

"We need to be looking for anyone – or any*thing* – that seems out of place, like they don't belong," Captain Marvel added.

Sometimes I'm the one who feels like I don't belong, Peter thought, remembering the loneliness he sometimes experienced.

"Sounds like you need to talk to someone who is very familiar with this station and everyone who lives on it," Peter said. "I know just the individual! Someone who knows this place like the back of his hand – well ... not hand, but paw...."

COSMO

*E*arly the next morning, Peter picked up Captain Marvel and they went to see **Cosmo** at his office. To Captain Marvel's credit, if she was surprised that the entire space station's security was the responsibility of a talking Earth dog, she didn't show it. But then again, she was probably used to seeing a lot of strange stuff during her work with the Avengers.

"Nice to make your acquaintance, Carol," Cosmo said. "May I call you Carol?"

"Uh, yes, feel free," Captain Marvel responded as she shook Cosmo's paw.

"Thank you. **Would you like some treats?**" Cosmo asked as he pushed a little dish of dog food across the desk to Captain Marvel.

"Oh, no, thank you," Captain Marvel replied politely.

"So. How can I help you?" asked Cosmo as he gnawed away on a bone.

But before Captain Marvel would say anything about the mission, she told Peter to ask his friend a few questions that only the real Cosmo would know the answer to.

"Where did I get this scratch last week?" asked Peter, pointing to a small abrasion on his arm.

"That probably happened when we were forced to give Rocket a bath," said Cosmo, "on account of those **RADIOACTIVE SPACE TICKS** that he picked up."

"It's true," Peter confirmed. "Rocket hates baths. He was scratching and biting the whole time."

AIN'T HAPPENIN'!

"Ask him one more, please," Captain Marvel requested. "Just to be sure."

"What game do you like to play in the hologram video game system?" Peter asked.

"THE ONE WHERE YOU GET TO CHASE A POSTMAN WITH ROCKET-BOOTS," Cosmo replied.

It was true. Peter had played that game with him before. It was pretty boring. You just chased the postman, caught him, and chased him again – over and over.

BAD DOG!

"That's Cosmo for sure," Peter confirmed.

"Now what's with all the strange questions?" asked Cosmo.

Captain Marvel filled him in about the missing SKRULL agent and the pieces of the Ultimate Nullifier.

"So you asked those questions to make sure a SKRULL hadn't taken my shape and was pretending to be me," Cosmo realized. "Very smart."

Cosmo took the SKRULL threat very seriously. He didn't want to be known as the head of security who let a dangerous criminal get away with one of the most powerful weapons in the universe. How would that look on his CV? Not very good!

Cosmo assigned his best security officer, **DEPUTY YON-ROGG**, to work with them. Yon-Rogg had lived on Knowhere for many years and knew everyone who made their home there. If someone was acting strangely, or something was out of place, Yon-Rogg would be able to spot it.

"We'll find your dirty SKRULL spy," said Yon-Rogg, who was a member of the alien race known as the **KREE**. The **KREE** didn't usually like the SKRULL very much, because there had been a long **KREE**–SKRULL War that left both sides angry and bitter.

As they set off to search for the spy, Cosmo warned Peter not to tell anyone about their mission. "The only advantage you have is that the SKRULL spy probably doesn't know that you're looking for them yet," Cosmo pointed out. "So don't mention it to anyone. Not even your closest friends, the other Guardians of the Galaxy. Because if word gets around, your SKRULL will probably run somewhere else."

Peter reluctantly agreed. He saw the importance of Cosmo's advice, but he didn't like the idea of hiding things from his best friends.

Soon, Star-Lord, Captain Marvel and Yon-Rogg set off looking  for anything suspicious. They looked everywhere. But after many hours of hard work, their search of Knowhere was going ... **NOWHERE**.

YOU MUST ENJOY LIVING HERE.

said Captain Marvel to Peter as they searched. "It's an extremely interesting place."

"I do...." replied Peter. "Well, usually I do. But recently I've been feeling homesick. It's been a long time since I left Earth, and sometimes I feel so different from everyone around me."

"I know what you mean," said Captain Marvel.

"You do?" asked Peter, surprised. "But you live on Earth."

"Yes, but ever since I absorbed **ALIEN DNA**, I've only actually been half human," explained Captain Marvel. "That's something some people on Earth don't understand. When they find out I'm not fully human, they always look at me a little differently, and I don't always feel like I fit in."

Before she could finish, Yon-Rogg ran up to the pair of earthlings, interrupting the conversation.

STAR-LORD, CAPTAIN MARVEL, COME WITH ME! I THINK WE'VE FOUND SOMETHING!

CHAPTER 5

Star-Lord raced down the street after Yon-Rogg and Captain Marvel. Just as he was passing the Celestial Boot's front door, the other Guardians of the Galaxy stepped out.

"Oh, Quill, there you are," said Rocket. "Just in time, come on! The Cosmic Circus just landed on the station, and we're going to go and see the robotic lion tamers."

"Wait.... Are they robotic lions that are being tamed, or are robotic tamers doing the taming?" asked Peter, confused.

"Both!" Drax shouted in delight. He was always up for a good robot sideshow act.

"I am Groot," Groot added.

"He's right," Rocket confirmed. "It is supposed to be awesome!"

"I'm more interested in the living tightrope walkers," remarked Gamora.

"Wait…. Are the tightrope walkers alive, or the tightrope itself?" Peter asked.

"Again, both!" Rocket shouted. "You've gotta come!"

Peter wanted to. A crazy alien circus with robotic lions and living tightropes…. Yeah, that sounded like it would be just up his alley. Plus, some hang time with the Guardians was never a bad thing.

But no … the fate of Earth, and even the

galaxy was in the balance. He had to work now and play later.

"Sorry, guys. I want to, but I just can't," Peter said reluctantly.

"Why not?" Gamora asked. "What do you need to do that's so important?"

"I bet I know what it is," Rocket said. "Another human from Earth came to the station last night, and now you would rather hang out with her instead of us."

Gamora gasped. **"Peter, is that really what it is?"**

"No...." Peter started. He was about to explain the whole situation, about the Skrull and the missing parts for the Ultimate Nullifier, but then he remembered the warning from Cosmo not to tell anyone about his secret mission. This also went for his best friends.

"It is good to see another earthling, but that's not why I can't hang out right now. It's just that **I'm...not...feeling...very... good,**" Peter lied. "I've been, like, throwing up everywhere and stuff. Something I ate maybe? I'm going to head back to the ship and rest in bed."

Rocket eyeballed him. **"Well, you are looking a little feverish, I guess."**

"Okay," Gamora said. "You go lie down and feel better."

"I am Groot," Groot agreed.

"Thanks, guys. Sorry to miss it," Peter said, and he waved and wandered away. But as soon as he was **around the corner** and out of view, he raced in the direction that Yon-Rogg and Captain Marvel had gone.

Later, as Gamora, Drax, Rocket and Groot stood in line to enter the Cosmic Circus rocket tent, they could look down to see most of Knowhere. The rocket tent was docked and hovering near the ceiling of the station, so anyone standing on the waiting platforms had a great view of the streets below.

"I hope Peter feels better soon," Gamora said.

"I am Groot," Groot remarked.

"What are you talking about, Groot?" Rocket asked his friend. "Quill's not down there. Didn't you hear him? He's back at the ship, trying to sleep off his bug."

But Groot insisted, pointing down to the streets of Knowhere below. Rocket, using his special **CYBERNETIC EYES**, zoomed in to see what Groot was trying to show them.

"Why that little...." he mumbled to himself. "Groot's right. That's Quill down there. He's standing at some warehouse. And sure enough, he's with Captain Marvel!"

Everyone was shocked! "But I thought he was supposed to be lying down in his ship," Drax remarked.

"Oh, he's lying all right," Rocket said. **"Lying to us, his so-called friends."**

"Oh, Peter...." Gamora murmured very sadly.

6

After leaving the Guardians at the Celestial Boot, Peter caught up with Yon-Rogg and Captain Marvel at a section of Knowhere that was mostly used for storage. All around them were old broken-down ships and pieces of large mining equipment that were smashed and rusting. *The perfect place for a* SKRULL *agent to hide out*, Peter thought.

The heroes finally came to a stop in front of an old warehouse that was practically falling down.

"Our security department intercepted chatter that some heavy-duty weapons were being smuggled through an **ILLEGAL TELEPORT NODE** set up in this warehouse," Yon-Rogg explained to the others. "Knowhere isn't a very large station, so there aren't that many illegal arms deals going down at any one time. The guy you're looking for HAS to be involved."

The three peered through the window.

"These two are SHI'AR," Peter said, naming the race of aliens he saw inside. "Not SKRULLS." SKRULLS look completely different. They are green and kind of **LIZARD-LIKE**.

"Yes, but your SKRULL is a shape-shifter," Yon-Rogg reminded them. "He could be disguised as a SHI'AR for all we know."

"True," Captain Marvel admitted.

Peter and his companions watched through the window as the two SHI'AR pulled in several large crates. **"The weapons MUST be in those crates,"** Yon-Rogg remarked.

The SHI'AR turned a button on a teleporter device, and as soon as it came on, they began pushing the crates through the portal that it created.

"This is happening right now!" Yon-Rogg shouted. "They're already teleporting the weapons out!"

"MOVE IN!" Captain Marvel shouted.

But the SHI'AR didn't have any plans to be captured. They fired blasters of their own and

EVERYONE JUMPED INTO
ACTION!

Captain Marvel flew at one of the SHI'AR, using her super powers to shoot bolts of energy from her fingertips. At the same time, Star-Lord and Yon-Rogg both attacked the other Shi'ar.

The first SHI'AR landed a blast on Captain Marvel that knocked her across the room, where she smashed into a pile of old equipment. Free of her attack, the SHI'AR pulled open one of the crates in front of him. The opened crate held a wide variety of exotic weapons, including some that looked like long tubes with little hoses on the end.

While the first SHI'AR pulled out the tube-weapons, the second SHI'AR kicked and punched at Yon-Rogg and Star-Lord with dangerously powerful blows!

"You're going to wish you just let us arrest you," said Star-Lord as he punched back at the second SHI'AR.

"I doubt that," said the first SHI'AR as he sprayed Star-Lord and Yon-Rogg with the strange tube-like weapon.

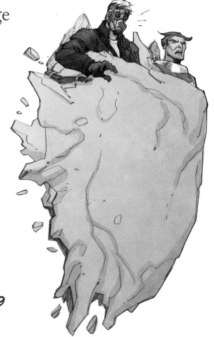

Star-Lord and Yon-Rogg were **splashed back** against the warehouse wall, where the fluid they were sprayed with hardened instantly into an unbreakable foam! No matter how much the two struggled, they couldn't break free.

"And I have something good planned for your friend," the SHI'AR said. He watched

as **Captain Marvel**

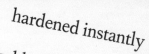

pulled herself from the pile of twisted metal where she'd landed and prepared to launch a new attack. "This is a teleport grenade," the alien said.

"When it goes off,
it'll teleport anyone
near it."

"Teleport them where?"

Peter asked desperately.

"Into the heart of a sun,"

the SHI'AR laughed.

"Say goodbye to your friend!"

He threw the
teleport grenade
right at Captain Marvel.

Oh, no!

Peter thought.

Captain Marvel's
going to be destroyed!

CHAPTER 7

Peter watched in horror as the SHI'AR criminal threw his teleport grenade at Captain Marvel. And because he couldn't move, there was nothing Star-lord could do to save his fellow hero. Or was there?

Peter's fingertips, the only little part of himself free from the foam, brushed across something in his pocket. It was one of the space

darts that Rocket had invented — the ones that used homing beacons to go wherever you told them to go, even if you threw them in the wrong direction.

That was it!

I've only got one chance, Peter thought.

Using his fingers, he quickly worked the space dart out of his pocket and weakly tossed it out — but not before telling it:

"Teleport grenade!"

The dart *BEEPED* and whooshed off.

74

Even though Peter had tossed it in the wrong direction, and only with fingertip force, it still shot straight for the target.

The dart caught up with the teleport grenade, slammed into it, and set it off in mid-air, before it had a chance to reach **Captain Marvel!**

The grenade burst into a ball of teleport energy. Luckily, it wasn't close enough to hit Captain Marvel but it struck the crates of **SHI'AR WEAPONS**

Instantly, they became sucked into the teleport ball and disappeared!

75

"Our weapons — NO!" the first SHI'AR shouted as he realized that all the illegal cargo had just been whisked into the heart of a sun – and all by his own grenade.

But he didn't have much time to be upset, because within seconds Captain Marvel had rushed over and delivered a devastating punch, knocking him out. Captain Marvel then made short work of the second SHI'AR and used her energy blasts to free Peter and Yon-Rogg from the trapping foam.

"Thank you, Star-Lord," Captain Marvel said to Peter. **"You saved my life."**

"You returned the favour," Peter replied. "If it wasn't for you, I'd still be stuck to that wall, and who knows what they would have done to me? So, thanks."

"Now that we've saved each other's lives," Captain Marvel said, "I think you can go ahead and start calling me Carol."

"And you can call me Peter," he said, smiling.

Within minutes, Cosmo arrived with more help from the security office, and the SHI'ARS' whole operation was cleaned up.

"So ..." said Cosmo, "did you get what you were after?"

"I think so," Yon-Rogg said. "All of the crates containing weapons were teleported into the heart of a sun. If the parts of the Ultimate Nullifier were in those crates, then they were destroyed."

"Yes ... *if* they were in there," said Captain Marvel. We unfortunately didn't see inside most of the crates, so we can't know for sure.

"Plus, we were looking for one SKRULL agent," Peter reminded them, "but these are two SHI'AR agents. We've examined their unconscious bodies, and they definitely are real SHI'AR, not SKRULLS disguised as SHI'AR."

"Yes," admitted Yon-Rogg, "but like I said before, Knowhere isn't *that* big. The odds that two sets of illegal weapons were being smuggled through here on the same day must be very high. We can't know for sure, but chances are that the stuff we were looking for was in those crates."

"Yeah, maybe..." Captain Marvel said, deep in thought.

"But if the nullifier parts were in there, where's our SKRULL agent?" Peter asked. "And why would he have given his cargo over to the SHI'AR?"

"**A tough dilemma,**" Cosmo admitted. "Maybe you completed your mission ... and maybe you didn't."

CHAPTER 8

*T*hat evening, after all the commotion of the day was over, Captain Marvel walked with Peter back to the ship.

"What are you going to do now?" Peter asked.

"I don't know," Captain Marvel said. "I know **YON-ROGG** thinks the pieces of the Ultimate Nullifier were destroyed, but how can I be sure? The fate of the Earth might depend on this."

"By morning, we'll probably be able to question those SHI'AR," Peter pointed out. "If they don't know anything about a SKRULL agent, then we probably have to keep looking."

"Agreed," Carol said as they reached the front door of Peter's ship. "No matter what we do tomorrow, I'm beat for the night. Good night, Peter."

GOOD NIGHT, CAROL.

THANKS AGAIN FOR YOUR HELP TODAY. I CAN SEE WHY THE GUARDIANS VALUE YOU SO MUCH.

BZZZZZZZZZZ ZZZZZZZZZ

Later, Peter was about to head to bed when there was a **BUZZ** at the ship's door. "Who is it?" Peter asked. Then he opened the door to find the rest of the Guardians outside.

ZZZZZZZZZZ

"Oh ... uh ... I was just about to get some sleep," Peter stuttered as he moved aside, letting the other Guardians through. "It's been a long day."

"A long day of lying in bed?" Gamora asked. **"I hope you're not still feeling ill."**

Ill? What was she talking about...? Oh, yeah.... Peter suddenly remembered his lie from earlier. He put his hand to his stomach as if it were hurting him. "I'm feeling a little better – "

"Stop there," Drax said. **"We know you lied about being sick."**

"I am Groot," Groot said, nodding.

"We saw you hanging out with Captain Marvel," Rocket reported.

"Oh," Peter said, surprised to be caught in his lie.

"If you didn't want to hang out with us, you could have just told us," Gamora said, clearly very hurt by Peter's deception.

"No, I did want to hang out with you," Peter assured them. "It's just that something came up and I couldn't tell you what it was."

WE CAUGHT YOU!

"I am Groot?" Groot asked.

"Yeah," Rocket agreed. **"Why not?"**

"I promised that I wouldn't tell anyone what I was doing," Peter tried to explain. He was feeling **backed into a corner** by this point. "So I had to make up that story about being sick. Really, I would much rather have gone to the circus with you guys."

"Peter," Gamora said, frowning, **"you know you can tell us anything."**

"Yeah, what was so important that you had to lie about it?" Rocket asked.

But Peter was stuck. It wasn't clear if they'd actually found the Ultimate Nullifier pieces yet, and the escaped SKRULL agent was still out there. In fact, it was even possible that one of the Guardians was kidnapped and trapped somewhere, and that one of the people in his ship right now was a SKRULL impostor. This whole mess wasn't over yet, so his promise to Cosmo still stood. He couldn't tell his friends anything.

"I ... I'd better not say," Peter replied. As he said it, he could see the hurt in his friends' eyes. They felt betrayed.

"I thought you were our friend, Peter Quill," Rocket said angrily. "I guess you never really know someone, do you? Come on, Guardians, let's get out of here."

The rest of the Guardians followed Rocket out of the door, leaving Peter alone. He felt terrible about keeping secrets from his friends. If only he could explain! Surely they'd forgive him if they knew the circumstances.

But there was nothing he could do about that now, so he went ahead and climbed into bed to finally get some rest.

That night, inspiration struck Peter! The next morning, bright and early, he burst into Cosmo's office, where Captain Marvel and Yon-Rogg were already speaking with the canine security chief.

"Stop everything!" Peter shouted. **"I know how to find the SKRULL agent!"**

"You do?" everyone asked as they jumped excitedly to their feet.

CHAPTER

9

"*T*ell us how to find him, Star-Lord!" Cosmo demanded as he, Yon-Rogg and Captain Marvel anxiously looked on.

"It was something Rocket said to me last night," Peter explained. "He said, 'You never really know someone.' That means that even though you've spent time with someone, there might still be things you don't know about them."

"Yes ... and?" Captain Marvel asked.

"Well, Captain Marvel is the one who told us there was a SKRULL, so it's obviously not her," Peter noted. "And when we first talked to Cosmo, we asked him questions that only he would know the answers to, so it's clearly not him – "

"Where is this going?" Yon-Rogg asked.

"It's going to you, Yon-Rogg," Peter said. "We never asked you any questions."

"I told you, he's one of my most trusted officers," Cosmo explained.

"Sure, you trust the real YON-ROGG," Star-Lord said, "but what if this is a SKRULL who has replaced your officer? What if the Yon-Rogg you know is being held prisoner somewhere, while this person lives his life?"

"Yon-Rogg isn't just my best officer, he's one of my best friends," Cosmo said. "Don't you think I'd know him?"

"SKRULLS are good mimics," Peter pointed out. "Think about it. He's the one who is trying to convince us that the Ultimate Nullifier must have been in those SHI'AR crates that were destroyed."

"THIS IS RIDICULOUS!"

shouted an outraged Yon-Rogg. "I think the Ultimate Nullifier pieces were in those crates because they probably were. Where else on the station would they be?"

"There's an easy way to solve this," Captain Marvel pointed out. "Cosmo, ask Yon-Rogg some questions that only he'd know the answers to."

"Okay ... Ronny, what did you get me for my birthday last year?" Cosmo asked.

"What? You're buying this?" Yon-Rogg asked Cosmo. "You've known me for years."

"Of course not," the dog assured him. "Just tell me what you got me last year. We'll prove Star-Lord wrong and be done with it."

"I'm not sure I even remember what I got you," Yon-Rogg protested.

"Oh, no, you'll remember this," Cosmo said, encouraging him. "Just think about it."

Yon-Rogg was quiet for a moment, as all eyes were on him. Was he really just trying to remember something ... or was it more than that? Finally, he said, "Well, Star-Lord is wrong. Because I'm not your average SKRULL.

I'M A SUPER

And in that moment Yon-Rogg trans-
formed into a **GREEN-SKINNED
ALIEN** with pointed ears and scales!
The other three jumped out of their chairs
with surprise.

SKRULL!"

Peter had never fought a SUPER SKRULL before, but he knew that just as on Earth there were human Super Heroes with special powers, on the planet of the SKRULLS there were individuals with exceptional abilities!

Moving incredibly quickly, the super SKRULL pounded Captain Marvel with a blast of **PURE FIRE** and knocked Cosmo away with a fist that turned into a giant hammer! Peter blasted the SUPER SKRULL, but before the lasers reached him, the alien Super Villain raised an invisible energy shield that deflected the shots.

The SUPER SKRULL laughed. "Tricking you was fun. I'm sorry that it's over. But that's okay.

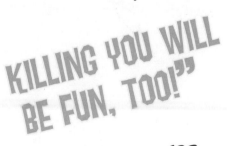

KILLING YOU WILL BE FUN, TOO!"

The SUPER SKRULL, still pinning Captain Marvel to the ground with fire, used his hammer-hand to slam Peter into the wall.

"I NEVER EXPECTED YOUR TINY BRAINS TO FIGURE IT OUT, EARTHLINGS."

"OOF!" The breath went out of Peter with the impact. He tried to get to his feet, but when he looked up, he saw that the giant hammer-hand was raised and about to come down on him again – for possibly the last time.

Groot doughnut?

CHAPTER 10

*J*ust before the Super Skrull's powerful hammer-fist fell on the already battered Peter, a giant wooden shield appeared above him! It took the heavy blow, protecting Peter.

Wait... that wasn't a shield. It was Groot!

"I am Groot," Groot shouted as splinters flew off his body!

Suddenly, the rest of the Guardians of the Galaxy burst into Cosmo's office.

"Hey, ugly!" Rocket said as he raised a hyper-blaster gun he'd just built. "I never thought I'd see a face as revolting as Drax's, but you take the biscuit!" Then he fired at the attacking alien.

The force of the blast knocked the SUPER SKRULL back, making him lose his aim. Now that he was no longer able to focus his fire blast on **Captain Marvel**. The Avenger was able to spring up and shoot blasts from her fingertips at him!

"Rocket's right!" Drax shouted. He launched himself into the air at the Super Skrull. **"You are uglier than me!"**

As Drax swung his blades at one side of the Super Skrull, Gamora came up on the other side, chopping with her sword!

"You mess with Star-Lord, you mess with all the Guardians of the Galaxy!" Gamora shouted.

Peter watched his friends in amazement. Even though he'd been so bad to his friends, avoiding them and lying to them, they still didn't hesitate to help him when he was in trouble.

Between the blows from Drax and Gamora and the blasts from Rocket and Captain Marvel, the Super Skrull was on the ground in seconds.

"Nighty-night," said Drax as he knocked the alien agent out.

Later, a quick search of Yon-Rogg's apartment turned up both the real Yon-Rogg, tied up in a closet, and also the pieces of the Ultimate Nullifier that Captain Marvel had come to Knowhere to find. With the Super Skrull now her prisoner, the mission was complete. **"The Earth is now safe — thanks to you, Peter, and to the other Guardians,"** Captain Marvel said.

"And thanks to you," Peter added, very gratefully.

"I'm headed back now to return these pieces to S.H.I.E.L.D. and Nick Fury," Captain Marvel said.

I KNOW YOU'VE BEEN MISSING EARTH AND FEELING HOMESICK. WHY DON'T YOU COME BACK WITH ME?

Peter smiled at the Avenger.

Nearby, the other Guardians, who had heard everything, turned and walked away.

"Well, that's it," Rocket said to the others. "We won't see Quill again."

"What do you mean?" Gamora asked. "Even if he goes with her, he'll come back soon, I'm sure."

"No way," Rocket said. "Once he gets comfortable on Earth, he'll have no reason to come back here again."

"It's bad for us to lose him from the team," Drax said, "but maybe it's what's best for him. He has been unhappy here lately."

Later, watching from afar, the Guardians saw Captain Marvel's ship leave the space dock and head out of Knowhere through one of the

skull-shaped station's eyeholes.

"Goodbye, you stinking meat-bag," Rocket said, waving to the ship. All of the Guardians lowered their heads. They would miss their friend.

IT WAS GOOD KNOWING YOU, QUILL, EVEN THOUGH YOU SMELLED LIKE A HUMAN.

"HEY, WHY ARE YOU GUYS ACTING SO WEIRD?"

said a voice behind them.

They turned. It was Peter!

"Quill, what are you doing here?" Drax asked.

"Yeah, we thought you were on that ship heading for Earth," Gamora added.

"What? Why would I be?" Peter asked.

"Because you were all home-sick and mopey and everything," Rocket pointed out.

"Well, true," Peter admitted, looking at them. "I'm sorry I kept secrets from you. But even though I haven't been a great friend, you all still jumped in and risked your lives to rescue me."

Peter gave them a significant look. **"And that ... is what a family does."**

"But ... but ... Peter...." Gamora stammered. "Don't you want to go home?"

"You know what I've finally figured out, Gamora?" Peter asked. **"I'm already home."**

They all smiled at each other.

"All right, enough with this mushy stuff," Rocket said, pretending like he was too much of a tough guy to be moved by Peter's words. "With that settled, let's go to the Orlani races!"

"I am Groot!" Groot shouted very excitedly.

That night, their favourite Orlani lost the race, but they didn't mind. They were together.